FB J930

04/21

...........p (2008), NHS Innovation (2011), NIHR Research Professorship (2013)

"*Has the bug bitten you? Are you curious? Curious to know how the universe evolved from the Big Bang? How matter arranges itself into objects ran*............................*lets,*"

and stars? Are you curious to know why all these things are the way they are?

"Science is good for the 'how' questions but does not necessarily have the answers on the 'why' questions. Can science and religion talk to each other? Enjoy this series and learn more about science and the enriching dialogue between science and faith."

PROFESSOR ROLF HEUER
Director General of CERN from 2009 to 2015
President of the German Physical Society and President of the
SESAME Council

"Here is a wonderful and wittily written introduction to science as the art of asking open questions and not jumping to conclusions. It's also an amusing excursion through evolution and anthropology which packs in a lot of learning with the lightest of touches. A much-needed antidote to the bludgeoning crudity of so much writing in both science and religion."

REVEREND DOCTOR MALCOLM GUITE
Poet, singer-songwriter, priest, and academic
Chaplain at Girton College Cambridge

THE CURIOUS SCIENCE QUEST

CAVE DISCOVERY

WHEN DID WE START ASKING QUESTIONS?

JULIA GOLDING

WITH ANDREW BRIGGS AND ROGER WAGNER

ILLUSTRATIONS BRETT HUDSON

LION
CHILDREN'S

Published by Lion Children's Books
an imprint of
Lion Hudson Limited
Wilkinson House, Jordan Hill Business Park,
Banbury Road, Oxford OX2 8DR, England
www.lionhudson.com/lionchildrens

ISBN 978 0 7459 7744 7
e-ISBN 978 0 7459 7758 4

First edition 2018

Acknowledgments

Scripture quotation p. 10 taken from The Authorized (King James) Version.
Rights in the Authorized Version are vested in the Crown. Reproduced by
permission of the Crown's patentee, Cambridge University Press.

A catalogue record for this book is available from the British Library

Printed and bound in the UK, May 2018, LH26

CONTENTS

Contents

INTRODUCTION

Life is full of big questions, what we might call ultimate questions.
Here are just a few of them:
- How did the universe begin?
- How will it end?
- Is there a God behind it, or is it the result of chance?
- Has science explained away the need for a Creator, as some people claim, or can you be a top scientist and still believe?
- Can having a faith even help some people to do well in their scientific research?

But perhaps the first question to ask is when and why did humans start to ask questions like this?
- When did we get bitten by the curiosity bug?

STOP BUGGING ME!

Our Time Travelling Guides

It's time to meet our guides to the ultimate questions.

Harriet is a tortoise. She was collected by Charles Darwin on his famous voyage on *The Beagle* (1831–36), when he explored the world and saw many things that led him to the Theory of Evolution. Harriet was brought back in his suitcase to England to be the family pet. Because she is a tortoise she can live for a very long time and is well over a hundred years old.

Harriet

Milton is a cat. He belongs to the famous twentieth-century physicist, Erwin Schrödinger, and inspired some of his owner's best ideas. Milton is not very good at making up his mind.

Milton

Curious Quest

Thanks to their owners, Harriet and Milton love science but they don't always agree. This is a good thing as when scientists argue they test out ideas on each other and develop new ones. Harriet and Milton have decided to go on a quest to find out the answers to as many ultimate questions as they can. In fact they are going to travel in time to see all the important events in the history of science.

In this series, you are invited to go with them. You can also look out for the Curiosity Bug hidden in some intriguing places and see how many you can count. Answer on page 127.

The Curiosity Bug

The works of the Lord are great,
sought out of all them that have pleasure therein

THE QUEST BEGINS

How did this adventure through time come about? Well, it all started with an argument... of course!

One day, Harriet and Milton bump into each other under the archway to a famous laboratory in the University of Cambridge.

"Isn't it odd, Harriet, to write those words over a door into a modern scientific laboratory?" says Milton.

"Oh? Why do you think it is odd?" asks Harriet.

"Obviously, because there's no proof of any god being involved in creation," says Milton. "Science and faith are completely different things. They don't go together."

Harriet thinks for a bit. "Are you sure of that?"

Milton licks his paw. "Me? I'm Schrödinger's Cat. I can't be sure of anything."

"But isn't it something that makes you wonder, Milton? I know I'd like to find out the answer. Is the idea of God just something humans made up and then dropped when they decided science explains everything, or can a religious faith still work alongside science?"

"Oh, Harriet, don't be silly. There's no way to find out."

"I think there is and I have an idea how we might do it. But for that, we've got to travel right back to the beginning. Let's go to your master's study."

Harriet and Milton arrive to find Professor Schrödinger away from home, but on his desk is a big black box.

Harriet taps the lid. "I heard your master once say that this is a very special box. It has a mystery inside."

Milton gives it a good sniff. It smells of starlight and dust. "What mystery?"

"It can be and not be at the same time," says Harriet.

Milton scratches his ear. "Huh?"

"I told you it was a puzzle! With a little modification, we can travel in it to be somewhere else in time."

Milton is not convinced. "You're saying it's a time machine? But I didn't think time travel was possible."

Not put off, Harriet climbs inside. "Don't you know that anything is possible for Schrödinger's cat and Darwin's tortoise, Milton? Come on, we have a date at an art gallery opening 35,000 years ago."

Milton hesitates. To be honest, he is scared of enclosed spaces.

"Are you really going to miss out on the adventure?" Harriet's voice calls from within the box.

Gathering his courage, Milton enters the time machine.

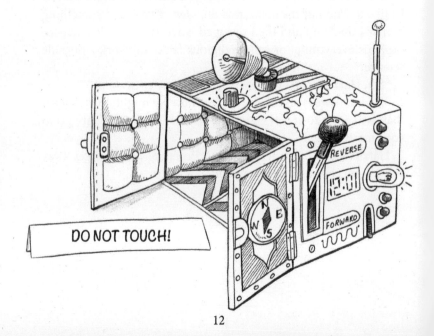

CURIOUS ABOUT
TIME TRAVEL?

Is time travel possible?

As far as we know, no one has come back from the future to tell us. If they did, there would be all sorts of dangers because they could change their past so they no longer existed. For example, they might stop their grandfather meeting their grandmother for the first time. So, would the time traveller then vanish the moment they stepped out of the time machine?

Harriet's Time Travel Method One: Go faster!

Time travel is possible – in theory. We know this thanks to a famous scientist called Albert Einstein (1879–1955).

In his theory of Special Relativity, he looked at space and time and realized that they were aspects of the same thing.

He called this "space-time".

He worked out that the closer you are moving to the speed of light (300,000 km per second), the slower time moves for you compared to those who aren't going at that speed.

Now here comes the mind-expanding stuff. Imagine you are heading off on a spaceship that can travel almost at the speed of light (99.5 per cent). You travel for five years. Time carries on as normal for your classmates on Earth but for you it is going much more slowly. When you get back, you've aged by five years, but they have aged by fifty! So if you were ten when you left, you'd get back at fifteen, while your friends would be sixty and thinking about retirement.

And, theoretically, according to the late British physicist Stephen Hawking, you could come back before you even take off, though he rather doubted this would ever happen!

Harriet's Time Travel Method Two: Jump in a black hole!

Albert Einstein worked out a second way to time travel in his other theory: General Relativity. The universe is full of gravitational fields. This is the "pull" force between matter and is stronger the bigger the object is, for example there is a strong "pull" force between planets and suns. The objects in the universe with the biggest gravitational fields are black holes. They are so dense that even light cannot escape their gravity, which is why they appear to be black.

Time passes more slowly for objects in gravitational fields than for objects far from them. This means that near a black hole time gets distorted.

Scientists (who get very excited about this kind of thing) wonder if there might be time distortions, or worm holes, in black holes that could act like short cuts to other parts of the universe.

But have you spotted the BIG problem? Remember what happened to light? Yes, you guessed it. You would have to survive the huge pull of the black hole and no one has worked out how to do that.

Both Harriet's Methods One and Two are ways of going more slowly into the future while others go at normal Earth time. No one (except Harriet and she is keeping it a secret) has yet worked out a way to go *back* in time. But that doesn't mean it isn't possible. Maybe you will find the answer if you become a scientist?

CAVE PAINTERS

Amazing! These are really old!

Into the caves: 26,000 years ago

The time machine lands far underground in the Chauvet Cave in south-west France. Harriet and Milton get out.

"When are we?" asks Milton, sniffing the air. "I think I can smell a dog."

"We are 26,000 years ago," says Harriet.

Milton looks puzzled. "But I thought you said we were going further back in time than that?"

"We are, but there's someone I'd like you to meet first," explains Harriet.

"Who's that?"

"The first known visitor to a kind of art gallery; though it was, of course, nothing like a modern one. It was a special place and very hard to get to; it might even have been secret. Modern explorers found a child's footprints and marks on the walls where she (or possibly he) made a trail so she didn't get lost. She came with the dog you can smell. We know this because we found its footmarks too."

"So she isn't from the same people who made the paintings?" asks Milton.

"No," says Harriet. "The painters lived almost ten thousand years before her, even further back than the ancient Egyptians are to us. So her coming here is a bit like a modern child going to see the pyramids."

Amazing! These are really old!

"Why do you think she's here?" whispers Milton.

"We can't be sure, but I bet she's curious," says Harriet, getting back into the time machine.

Milton jumps in after her, eager to get on with the quest.

"I want to see the pictures being drawn. How much further back do we have to go?"

"To around 35,000 years," says Harriet, setting the dial.

"Is that the beginning of history?" asks Milton.

"Oh no, that goes back much, much further. Think of it this way..."

Harriet's Calendar Timeline of Earth

Imagine Earth's history as a calendar year.

DECEMBER

15 Party!	16	17	18	19
20	21	22	23	
25	26 Dinosaurs extinct	27	28	29 Primates appear
30	31 Human-like creatures			

- Our planet begins on 1 January.
- Life in the form of bacteria appears around February or March.
- There's a long wait until multi-celled plants start growing in October.
- More complex animals, such as sea-living trilobites, arrive in November.
- In late November, fish swim into view and, by the beginning of December, the first animals start to leave the seas for land.

- Dinosaurs have their party in the middle of December but are extinct around 26 December.
- Primates appear, with monkeys swinging into action on 29 December, followed a day later by apes.
- Human-like creatures arrive around midday on 31 December.
- Modern humans only appear for the last twenty minutes of the day, moving out of Africa into Europe and Asia six minutes ago, then to America after that. Farming began just over sixty seconds ago and the Christian era started in the last fifteen seconds.
- Those of us alive today have only lived for a fraction of the last second before midnight on 31 December.

Into the caves: 35,000 years ago

Feeling braver now, Milton looks out of the porthole in the box and sees time rushing by in a streak of stars.

"Are we nearly there yet?" he asks.

"Yes, we are," says Harriet, opening the door.

I love what she's done with the old place.

"Did you know, Milton, that after the child visitor came with her dog a landslide cut off the entrance? So the next people to see these paintings arrived in 1994," says Harriet.

OPENING TIMES FOR
CHAUVET CAVE

35,000 TO 26,000 YEARS AGO:
OPEN

THEN CLOSED FOR REPAIRS

RESTRICTED OPENING HOURS
FROM 1994

All visitors enter at their own risk

Management does not accept
responsibility if you are eaten by bears

"When the cave explorers cleared a path inside they found more than a thousand images," Harriet continues. "Some use perspective tricks that we thought only modern artists understood. Others are in big panels where it looks like the animals are running. This one is 15 m long! See it now, Milton, in the flickering light of the torches – don't the horses, lions, and bison look like they're moving?"

"It's brilliant, Harriet! It's like a cinema for cave people!"

Harriet smiles. "Or maybe these big pictures had even more meaning for them than that?"

"So what are the paintings for?"

"I don't speak their language to ask them," explains Harriet, "and they can't write things down, so we have to make our best guess."

INTRODUCING

THE HYPOTHESIS

ALSO KNOWN AS AN IDEA TO BE TESTED,
SOMETIMES KNOWN AS TODAY'S BEST GUESS!

Scientists and other experts share a method that helps them in their research. This is what they call a hypothesis. The word in Greek means "under" (hypo) and "placing" (thesis), so it works out as an _underlying_ idea or foundation.

(Not to be confused with underwear.)

Once a scientist has found out all the facts they can about a subject, they put together as full a picture as possible. They then argue as to who is right.

As you can see, some guesses are better than others. The experts use their hypothesis, or best guess, to guide them as they keep on looking for the missing information that will close the gaps. Sometimes the pieces raise even more questions and lead to further hypotheses, but that is all part of the fun of their Curious Quest through science.

Harriet and Milton get back into the time machine.

"So how are we going to find out what the paintings mean?" asks Milton.

Harriet retreats into her shell for a moment and comes back out with one of her hypotheses that she carries around inside her home.

"Here's a hypothesis I prepared earlier. Read this, Milton."

Harriet's Hypothesis (and how to make a best guess about cave paintings)

Cave pictures painted many thousands of years ago have meanings. We have two ways of going about finding our puzzle pieces to discover possible meanings.

Number One

Keep looking for more. Many of the cave paintings have been discovered very recently. There are probably more sites waiting to be uncovered by an intrepid explorer. The more pictures we have to compare to each other, the better our theory will be.

Number Two

Find paintings from other living cultures that might serve the same purpose.

"What do you want to do first?" asks Harriet.

"Go looking for more old pictures!" exclaims Milton.

Harriet laughs. "Europe is a good place to start. You could say it is the cave painters' hot spot!"

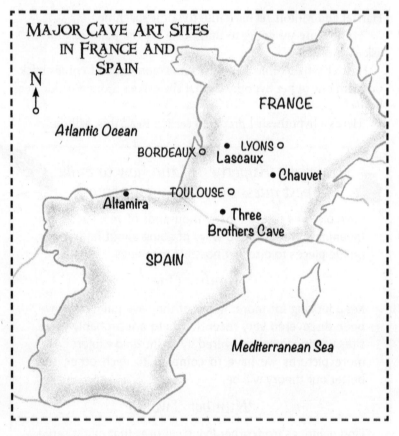

MAJOR CAVE ART SITES
IN FRANCE AND
SPAIN

N

FRANCE

Atlantic Ocean

BORDEAUX o   • LYONS o
          Lascaux
              • Chauvet

          TOULOUSE o
• Altamira
              • Three
          Brothers Cave

SPAIN

Mediterranean Sea

"So, Milton, now we've listed all the major caves found so far, what do you think about cave paintings?" asks Harriet.

"I think they're amazing," says Milton, washing his tired paws. "I've been making a list of the kind of subjects cave people liked painting and comparing them to what you see in most modern art galleries. Do you want to see?"

MILTON'S TOP FIVE FAVOURITES

CAVE PAINTERS FROM OVER 10,000 YEARS AGO	ARTISTS FROM THE LAST 500 YEARS
1. Hunting lions	1. Bowls of fruit
2. Bison	2. Pretty ladies
3. Galloping horses	3. Dead birds
4. Animal-headed people	4. Fat rich gentlemen
5. Handprint patterns	5. Chubby cherubs

Milton passes Harriet a second piece of paper.

"I've also made a guide as to how they did it." He rubs his paws vigorously. "This paint is so difficult to get off!"

Harriet gives him a hard stare. "You didn't leave a drawing behind did you? We can't confuse scientists by messing with the timeline."

"Well…" Milton looks very guilty.

"Milton! We'll have to go back and tidy up!"

MILTON'S GUIDE:
HOW TO BE A CAVE PAINTER

- First, think why you want to make a painting.
- Then take a perilous journey deep into a cave system. Don't forget a torch!
- Scrape the clay from the wall to make a white background.
- Outline your shape with charcoal.
- Mix charcoal with limestone so you can rub it into your shape.
- Finally, add fine detail like eyes with a pointy tool.
- For variety, you might want to blow ochre dust (an orange-red colour) around your hand to leave a pattern.
- Stand back and admire.

You can't leave until you've got it right!

A curious timeline of cave art

(Dates are all "years ago", c. = circa = around)

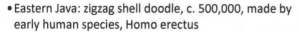

- Eastern Java: zigzag shell doodle, c. 500,000, made by early human species, Homo erectus
- Arrival of Homo sapiens (modern humans), c. 260,000
- South Africa: Blombos Cave artist's studio, c. 100,000
- Israel: Es Skhul Cave, oldest burial with grave goods, c. 90,000
- Blombos Cave criss-cross stone, c. 77,000
- Australia: Arnhem rock shelter handprints, c. 60,000?
- Indonesia: Sulawesi hand stencils and pig deer painting, c. 40,000
- Chauvet, France: c. 35,000
- Germany: Höhlenstein-Stadel Cave, lion-headed statue, c. 35,000
- Gower Peninsula, Wales: "Red Lady of Paviland" burial, c. 33,000
- Namibia: Apollo 11 Cave, oldest cave painting in Africa, c. 27,000
- Czech Republic: Pavlov ivory face, oldest human portrait? c. 27,000
- Namibia: "White Lady of Tsiah", c. 27,000
- Lascaux, France: c. 18,000
- Altamira, Spain: c. 14,000
- Nevada, USA: rock etchings, c. 14,000
- France: Three Brothers Cave, c. 13,000

Do you see what I see?

Milton is very impressed by his tour of cave paintings but still has many questions that need answering.

"I think I would have liked to be a cave artist," he admits. "Though I would have drawn lots more lions. But we still haven't really answered the question. What were the painters thinking when they made them?"

Harriet wonders how best to explain.

"When you and your friends look at a picture, do you all respond to it the same way?" she asks.

"Of course not," says Milton.

"So what does that tell you?" asks Harriet. "Remember where we found them and how much care they took creating their special effects."

Milton ponders this for a minute. "I think it means that they really had to want to make these pictures. It isn't easy to get into some of the caves and they'd have to bring their paints with them, not to mention torches for light. I think they were inspired to do it."

"Exactly!" says Harriet. "That's our best guess – they were inspired to make big pictures because they were having complex ideas about their world and their place in it.

"But scientists didn't always think the prehistoric cave people could see the world in a complex way, let alone produce paintings. If we go back to the nineteenth century, experts expected to find a very different kind of ancestor."

👍 (Mostly) Wrong Ideas Number 1 👎

What did our first ancestors think about?

According to historians in the nineteenth century, not a lot.

When the cave paintings were discovered in Europe, historians had a problem. Many had only just accepted Charles Darwin's Theory of Evolution (1859) that argued that humans are descended from an ape ancestor. They reasoned that early people therefore had to be less evolved versions of us. That meant our ancestors wouldn't have had complicated ideas or skills, such as making pictures and statues or clever tools. As the evidence mounted that they were wrong, historians rapidly had to change their minds. Our ancestors were a lot more intelligent and curious about the world much earlier than had been thought. And the people who found the evidence? The majority of the main finds were made by children just like you.

Kids v historians

Round 1: Ding, ding!

1879, Altamira, northern Spain: Maria de Sautola is playing in a cave on her father's estate. The eight-year-old often comes here with her dad and they have dug up all kinds of tools, pottery, shells, and teeth belonging to prehistoric people. But today she decides to go a little further. She crawls into a side chamber that's too low for adults and finds an amazing collection of paintings. "Look, Papa, oxen!" she calls.

> These are too good so they can't be the work of primitive ancestors. FAKE!

Round 2: Ding, ding!

1895, La Mouthe in the Dordogne, France: A farmer clears the entrance of a cave. Four boys go exploring into the cave system and find painted bison on the wall. The pictures have to be really

> Huh? How did these get here?

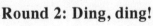

old as the rocks blocking the entrance had not been moved since the Stone Age.

Round 3: Ding, ding!

1901, two other cave systems in the Dordogne: Paintings are discovered with stalactites growing over them. Stalactites are rock formations made over thousands of years by the slow deposit of minerals as water drips on the cave floor. This meant the paintings beneath had to be even older.

Child explorers continue to lead the way

The finds didn't stop there.

Round 4: Ding, ding!

October 1912, Ariege, France:
A super-team, containing the Bégouën brothers –
Max, Louis and Jacques – and their friend,
Francois Camel, explore a local cave
called Tuc d'Audoubert. This is
how they did it...

I GIVE UP.
I was wrong.
The kids are
right.

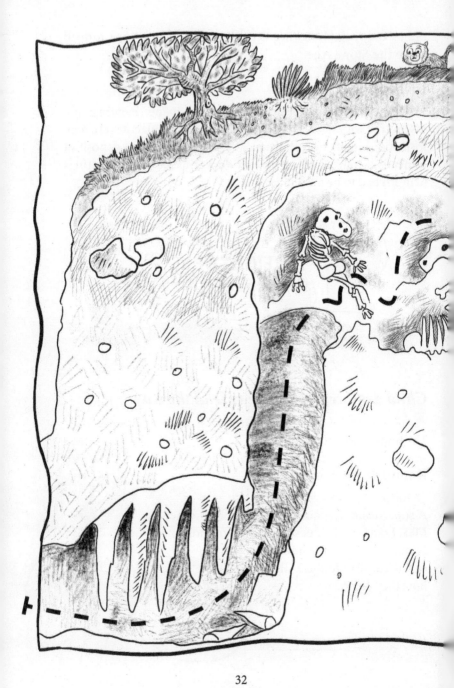

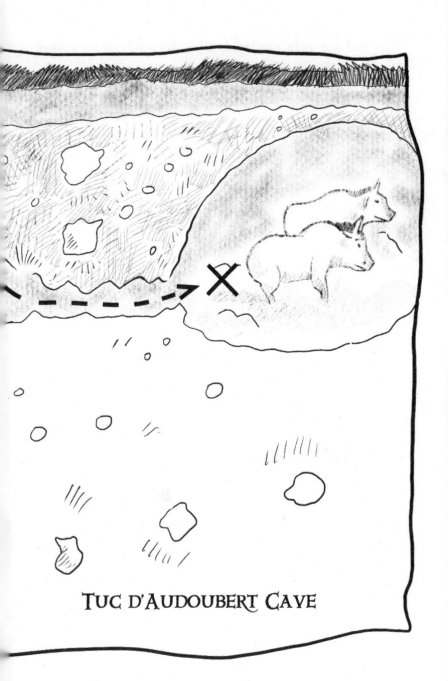

TUC D'AUDOUBERT CAVE

They find statues of two bison. Their dad sends off an excited telegram to the experts.

TELEGRAM

Guess what: prehistoric humans made models in clay!!!!

OK, I admit it. I don't know everything.

Round 5: Ding, ding!

July 1914: The super-team are at it again. They go down a pothole on the opposite side of the hill and find a huge cavern, now called the Three Brothers Cave after them. Halfway down there is an altar-like structure with a lion carving. Objects have been left there, stuck to the walls, possibly some kind of offering. At the far end is another chamber with lots of wall drawings, including a big one of a part-human, part-animal figure with antlers. Could it be a wizard? A god? A story?

Nobody knows exactly what it represents but it is clear it meant something powerful to the people who first looked at it. It was getting harder for historians to maintain that early humans had no clever thoughts about their place in the world. Maybe the images were even part of an early religion?

What do you think it meant?

CURIOUS CULTURES

Graduation day in North America

"So now, thanks to the young cave explorers, we've got lots more prehistoric paintings to look at, but we're still guessing as to what they mean," says Milton.

Harriet smiles. "I'm glad you pointed that out. It's time to go on the second part of our quest: to find the closest matches in cultures that can still remember why their ancestors drew the pictures."

"Great!" Milton runs after her as she boards the time machine. "What do I have to pack?"

"Sunglasses and sunscreen. It's a lot hotter than these French caves where we're going. First stop, Alabama in the south-east of the USA."

When Harriet and Milton arrive, they find themselves in a forest in the Appalachian mountains. They ask for directions from an elder of the Native American people of the region.

"You want to see our pictures?" the elder asks.

"We want to understand why they were made," explains Milton. He curls up on the man's lap for a stroke while Harriet sunbathes.

"Well now, I don't know what they all mean because some of them were made 6,000 years ago, but I have a good idea how they were done. You see, I asked my grandfather if I could be a cave artist too and this is what he told me…

"So the pictures have a spiritual meaning for your people," asks Milton. "They're not serving a practical purpose, like a record of hunts, a teaching tool or menu of things to eat?"

The elder chuckles. "I'm sorry to laugh, little cat, but what you are saying doesn't make sense to me. We don't think of spiritual things being separate from practical. Of course, these pictures have a practical purpose! They help bind our people together, in the same way our songs and our stories do. Sometimes they are like a graduation ceremony. When American young people leave high school, they make speeches and throw their hats in the air; we go on vision quests and draw what we see – that's how we know we've grown up."

"So, perhaps," muses Milton, "that's what some of the cave painters were doing all those thousands of years ago, marking the moment they became an adult?"

"Maybe," agrees the Elder. "But we'll never know for certain."

"That's OK, I'm used to uncertainty," says Milton.

A mix-up in southern Africa

"I hope you enjoyed meeting the elder in America," says Harriet, starting up the time machine, "because I'd like you to see some more old paintings, but this time from southern Africa."

"Happy to!" says Milton, admiring his reflection in the porthole glass. He is very pleased by the feathered headdress their Native American friend has given him as a souvenir. "Will there be lions?"

Harriet checks her map of the world to make sure she can find Namibia, in the south-west of Africa. "Possibly if we're lucky. But this visit is also about how wrong experts can be with their best guesses."

"Oh, I like to see that. I'm so often wrong, I find it reassuring brainboxes can be too."

👍 (Mostly) Wrong Ideas Number 2 👎 "The White Lady of Brandberg"

Harriet leads Milton to a cave painting in a rock shelter on Brandberg Mountain, the tallest peak in Namibia. "This picture is about 2,000 years old. Tell me what you think it shows."

Milton squints at the faded figures in the painting. "It looks like a hunting scene – people chasing four-legged creatures, like antelope. One of the people has a white bow and arrow and has white legs."

"And if I told you that when the first Europeans saw this, they thought that person with the bow and arrow was a lady, would you be surprised?" asks Harriet.

"I would," says Milton. "Did they know what they were talking about?"

"They should've done. One of them was the leading expert who had studied many of the cave paintings we've already visited in France – a man called Henri Breuil."

"Later," explains Harriet, "experts rejected this theory and decided the figure was probably a medicine man of the Bushmen ancestors leading a ritual, not a hunt. When you look closely, you can see that one of the animals, an oryx, actually has human back legs. It does show you how wrong even the experts can be."

MEET THE SCIENTIST

HENRI BREUIL, FATHER OF PREHISTORY

- Lived: 1877–1961
- Number of jobs: 2 (priest and artist)
- Influence (out of 100): 80 (brought back sketches of cave paintings he studied that were deep underground and inaccessible to ordinary people)
- Right? (out of 20): 16 (first to study the Lascaux paintings and work out the sequence of prehistoric cultures so we know roughly who did what when)
- Helpfully wrong? (out of 10): 0 (claimed the White Lady was done by European visitors because he didn't think the African Bushmen were advanced enough to make art.
- Interesting fact (out of 10): (his neighbours in Paris nicknamed him "the arrogant old priest" for thinking he was always right.)

Abbé Breuil! Cave-buster!

👍 (Mostly) Wrong Ideas Number 3 👎

Cave explorers haven't been very good at guessing the gender of their finds. In 1823 Reverend William Buckland found an ancient burial in a cave in Wales. The bones were stained red with ochre and buried with shell jewellery. He believed the world was only a few thousand years old so guessed the remains were Roman, and female because "she" had a necklace. Carbon dating later showed she was a "he" and much, much older. In fact, Buckland had found one of the oldest burials in Western Europe from 33,000 years ago.

That's no lady. That's the chief!

👍 (Mostly) Wrong Ideas Number 4 👎

People studying the cave paintings in modern times have also done more harm than good, often with the best intentions. The White Lady of Brandberg suffered rapid fading because visitors would throw water at it to make the colours come out more clearly. All that did was wash the paint away more quickly!

And the paintings in the famous Lascaux caves have been put at risk by the introduction of air conditioning in 2000 and powerful lights to be switched on for special visits. These proved to be the perfect growing conditions for mould which is spreading across half of the pictures. The problem hasn't been fixed but the caves have been closed to visitors, so that should help.

The old lady and the !gi

"But we can't leave the Namibian rock paintings without following the exciting story of the old lady and the !gi," says Harriet.

"Why are you making that clicking sound?" asks Milton. "Have you got a pebble stuck in your throat?"

Harriet gives him a reproving look. "No, I'm speaking /Xam. The ancient people of the Kalahari desert used clicks as part of the way they spoke, just like many other languages that still survive in this part of the world. Anthropologists learned the language, worked out a way to write it down, then collected the traditional stories of the /Xam."

Anthropologist: a person who studies other cultures. From Greek *anthropos* "human" and *logia* "study". (Not to be confused with a chiropodist, a person who looks after feet.)

A VISIT TO THE CHIROPODIST

"The anthropologists discovered that the /Xam saw the world as full of an invisible spiritual energy which they called !gi. They believed it was particularly strong in an animal called the eland, that appeared in many of their pictures. As the /Xam didn't hunt the eland for meat, these weren't hunting paintings. Something else was going on."

"So was there a connection between !gi power and their pictures?" wonders Milton.

"Yes, because something really exciting happened last century to cast new light on the subject. One group of anthropologists took an old lady, whose father had been a !gixa, or person full of !gi, to see some of the pictures he had painted long ago. She was so delighted to see the paintings again after many years that she started to dance in front of the images and held out her hands to them. She explained that her people, the /Xam San, believed that the pictures held spiritual power that could be drawn if you danced this way. You could use the energy for healing, rainmaking, and fighting evil spirits. The most sacred ceremony was when the San would dance and enter a trance so they could ask for healing energy to help the sick."

Milton holds up a paw experimentally. "So it's like a tribal power station and sacred place all in one."

"Yes. And when scientists examined what was in the paint, they found eland blood mixed in, which makes sense because they thought that animal had the most !gi."

"I'VE GOT !GI AND IT'S MULTIPLYING...'CAUSE THE POWER YOU'RE SUPPLYING – IT'S ELECTRIFYING!"

HOW TO MAKE /XAM PAINT – A POWERFUL BREW!

First go on a quest to find your colours – to the top of a mountain if you want to find ochre. Your colours are...

- ochre (red)
- manganese (black)
- charcoal

Then use the following binding agents...

- egg white
- milk
- eland blood

Milton checks his paws for signs of !gi. "So the pictures we saw in the caves in Europe might be the result of a quest by their equivalent of !gixa, special people like that old lady's father. They were painted to pass on power to others in the community."

"Maybe. But we mustn't forget that we are only guessing. There is a danger in playing "culture snap" with things from very different places. Remember the White Lady of Brandberg and the Red Lady of Paviland!"

SNAP!

"Right. Got it. So where to next?" asks Milton.

"Down Under. We're going to visit the first people to move to Australia: the Aboriginals. And I've got another wrong idea for you."

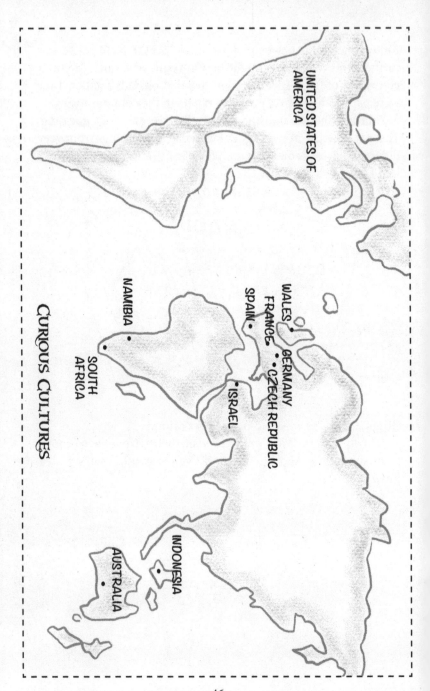

CURIOUS CULTURES

UNITED STATES OF AMERICA

WALES
FRANCE
SPAIN
GERMANY
CZECH REPUBLIC
ISRAEL

NAMIBIA
SOUTH AFRICA

INDONESIA
AUSTRALIA

👍 (Mostly) Wrong Ideas Number 5 👎

The ancestors of the Aboriginal people arrived in Australia around 65,000 to 60,000 years ago. They were able to come across land bridges from South-east Asia thanks to lower sea levels at that time in Earth's history, but they would have also had to make perilous journeys on rafts hopping from island to island.

People from Europe only discovered Australia in 1606. When white settlers started arriving in the nineteenth century they found pictures drawn on rocks by Aboriginal artists. They immediately leapt to the wrong conclusions.

Thunder down under

Harriet and Milton walk carefully across the rocky desert landscape.

"I don't want to make the same mistake," says Milton. "Let's ask someone who knows about it first-hand."

They find an elderly Aboriginal woman sitting in the shade of a rock shelter.

"Please would you tell us about the pictures your ancestors drew on the rocks," asks Harriet politely.

The old lady nods. "These hand stencils are the oldest and could have been made when my people first arrived in the land. Maybe they brought the idea of decorating walls with them from the places they once lived before that? Many of our pictures are about the Dreaming. That is the old time of the Ancestor Beings who emerged from the Earth's crust at creation.

"The Ancestor Beings were creatures and plants who were also part human. They created the landscape you see around you with their journeys, as well as all of the things in the physical world. Some of their spirits turned into rocks, or trees, or became part of the landscape. These are our sacred places and must be approached carefully. You can't move the pictures we draw from their place because that would destroy their meaning. Like chapters in a book they need to be read in the right order."

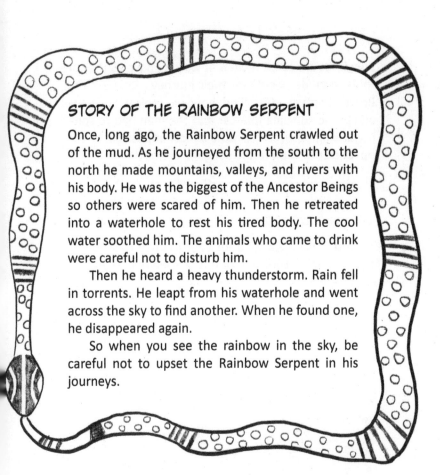

STORY OF THE RAINBOW SERPENT

Once, long ago, the Rainbow Serpent crawled out of the mud. As he journeyed from the south to the north he made mountains, valleys, and rivers with his body. He was the biggest of the Ancestor Beings so others were scared of him. Then he retreated into a waterhole to rest his tired body. The cool water soothed him. The animals who came to drink were careful not to disturb him.

Then he heard a heavy thunderstorm. Rain fell in torrents. He leapt from his waterhole and went across the sky to find another. When he found one, he disappeared again.

So when you see the rainbow in the sky, be careful not to upset the Rainbow Serpent in his journeys.

"The pictures and stories are our way of understanding the world," the old lady tells Harriet and Milton. "But they also help us make journeys of hundreds of miles because we record the landmarks in each location of the tale. The stories also tell you that you must do some things the right way. You must climb the great red rock Uluru by a certain path or you will anger the Ancestors. We also have to keep singing the songs so our land stays alive.

"These connections between stories and pictures are called songlines."

Songlines are to be recited at walking pace as they are tools to guide people on their journeys. One explorer, Bruce Chatwin, described how he took a local man along one songline in a car and the man had to speed up his singing until it became almost impossible to keep up. Better to explore the songline on foot!

TRY THIS AT HOME

Can you make a songline for your journey to school or a favourite place? Look out for the local landmarks and make up some stories to go with special spots along the way.

Do you think someone else could follow your songlines?

Back in the time machine, Milton draws up a list of what he has learned.

MILTON'S BEST GUESSES: WHAT DID CAVE PAINTING MEAN?

- Prehistoric graduation rite
- Pictures for shared stories
- Source of spiritual power
- Way of getting into contact with natural world and ancestors
- A kind of map or satnav
- Artistic experimentation
- Reflection on painter's place in world
- Menu and warning – what to hunt and what hunts us!

"That's what I've learned," says Milton. "What about you, Harriet?"

"I had two thoughts as we were travelling," says Harriet. "I think the pictures show us that the human brain had reached a point all across the world where it could think and communicate using symbols very early on. The second is that making pictures and sculptures go hand in hand with developing complex tools, like the abalone shell used as an artist's palette. This was found in the Blombos Cave in South Africa and dates from 100,000 years ago."

"So when did humans start to think this way?" wonders Milton.

"Really long ago," says Harriet. "You'll be shocked."

"I won't," Milton replies, huffily.

Harriet smiles. "Oh yes, you will. Because it may not be humans who started it."

Extreme Time Travel!

Harriet has her head deep in the time machine engine.

"What are you doing?" asks Milton, as springs and bolts zip past his ears.

"We have to go back further than I've ever taken the time machine before if we want to meet the creatures who first started thinking complex thoughts," explains Harriet. "I don't want to breakdown somewhere in the middle of the last few million years."

"And are we staying in Australia?" asks Milton, "I haven't met any kangaroos yet."

"The kangaroos will have to wait; this time we're going to Africa," says Harriet.

Milton looks confused. "Why are we going there?"

"Because that is where the human story starts," says Harriet. "Why don't you have a look at this chart? It shows us what the fossils found so far suggest about human origins."

Milton examines the chart she has pinned to the wall. "It looks complicated."

"It is, and there's a lot we still don't know. But pay special attention to the two breakaway points: first when apes, or what experts call *hominids*, split from other animals; and then when the human species, which all start with the word *homo*, broke off from apes. They are the key moments."

A FAMILY PORTRAIT TIMELINE
Harriet's Best Guess about Human Origins

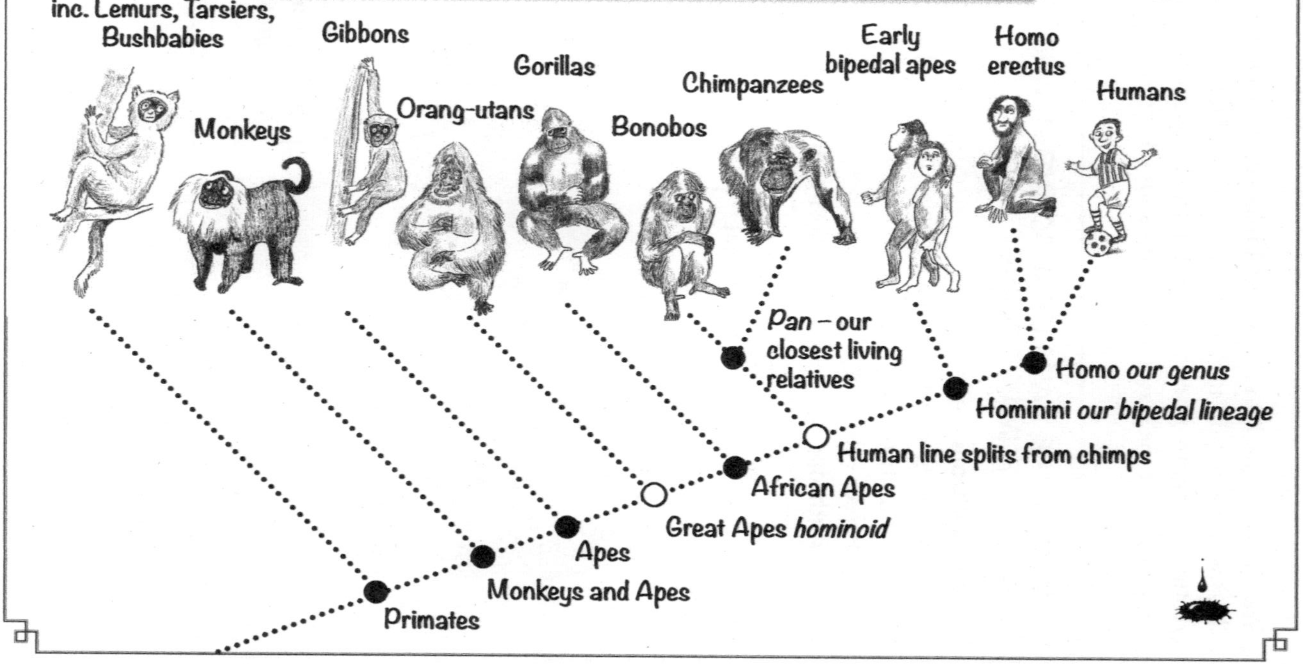

Prosimians inc. Lemurs, Tarsiers, Bushbabies

Monkeys

Gibbons

Orang-utans

Gorillas

Bonobos

Chimpanzees

Early bipedal apes

Homo erectus

Humans

Homo our genus

Hominini our bipedal lineage

Human line splits from chimps

Pan – our closest living relatives

African Apes

Great Apes *hominoid*

Apes

Monkeys and Apes

Primates

"We will come back to this when I take you to meet my master, Charles Darwin, and look at how it links to Bible stories about creation," explains Harriet.[1] "But for the moment we are in for some extreme time travel. Hold onto your whiskers!"

WHAT'S THE NAME OF A SCIENTIST WHO STUDIES HUMAN ORIGINS?

Paleoanthropologist.
That's a long word but much easier when you break it down into its parts:

Paleo – ancient
Anthropologist – human researcher

---

[1] You can follow that adventure in Book 5, Victorian Voyages!

HOW DO ANTHROPOLOGISTS DO THEIR RESEARCH?

1 Find your site	2 Listen to the locals	3 Dig very carefully
4 Record what you've found	5 Remove fossils and send to lab	6 Examine with special machines

41

"So which one of these ancient creatures started thinking?" asks Milton.

"That's a puzzle, isn't it?" laughs Harriet. "Let's go back and see. For that we have to return to Africa because that was the cradle for all the ape species. Apes emerged around 15 million years ago. Humans developed around 7 million years ago. Since then, there have been a number of human species, some dying out, some becoming part of human genetic inheritance."

WHAT IS GENETIC INHERITANCE?

Information about things such as our hair, skin, and eye colour are passed on from our parents through DNA.

DNA contains genes and is found in the nucleus of each cell. DNA is organised in bigger units called chromosomes. They travel in pairs.

Hi, I'm deoxyribonucleic acid, but you can call me DNA.

Sorry, I'm saving a seat for my buddy.

Chromosomes pass on instructions inside the cells of the embryo, the name for a human being in the womb when it's still very tiny.

I think I'll have black hair, brown eyes, freckles, and big feet.

Africa: 3 million years ago

The engine of the machine is running hot by the time Harriet and Milton arrive in the distant past. As they step out, they come across a landscape that is a mixture of trees and plains. A group of ape-like creatures are sitting together in the shade.

"See that one in the tree over there?" asks Harriet, pointing to a young male.

Milton looks over. "What about him?"

"His skeleton will be dug up in 1924 by an expert called Raymond Dart," says Harriet. "That ape is going to give the name to this species, the southern ape, or Australopithecus which means exactly the same thing but in Latin. Dart will suggest the skeleton to be an ancestor of humans."

"Why will he think that?" wonders Milton.

"Mainly because of two adaptations. These apes can walk on two feet and have smaller canine teeth so they are a step away from other apes that humans aren't so closely related to, like gorillas," explains Harriet.

"How will Dart know that if he won't have been able to travel back in time like we have?"

Harriet smiles. "It's all in the bones, Milton. If Dart and other experts find enough fossils, they can work out how the hips worked and that tells them if the species is adapted to walk on two legs or not."

"That's clever," says Milton, looking impressed.

MEET THE SCIENTIST

RAYMOND DART

- Lived: 1893–1988
- Number of jobs: 1 (fossil expert)
- Influence (out of 100): 70 (discovered the southern ape and suggested that its skull was closer in size to a human than most ape species so was more closely related to humans)
- Right? (out of 20): 20 (the southern ape's other bones told him that this species was adapted to walk on two legs)
- Helpfully wrong? (out of 10): 0 (most experts dismissed his claims because the fossil was from a child and they claimed he needed an adult specimen to prove his theory)
- Interesting fact (out of 10): 7 (he received the skull that gave him his breakthrough as he was getting ready to go to a wedding and the bridegroom had to drag him away so they would be on time – Dart didn't like to be separate from his skull after that, although his wife left it in a taxi once and it had to be rescued!)

Waiting for someone?

Drive on, I've got no body to go with me.

What is a fossil?

"Can you explain something to me, Harriet?" asks Milton.

"I'll try," says Harriet.

"What is a fossil?"

I'M PETRIFIED!

"You probably have seen one in a museum," says Harriet.

Milton nods. "Yes, often."

"What you're looking at is the impression or what's left of a plant or animal embedded in rock," explains Harriet. "We find it in petrified form – that means it has turned to stone."

Milton looks puzzled. "What do you mean by impression?"

I hope I made a good impression on you!

Harriet thinks for a moment. "Like footprints on soft soil. Fossil hunters have found dinosaur footprints, left millions of years ago. If the conditions are right, these can get quickly covered up by sediment or ash fall from a volcano before they can be washed away. Then they might be preserved for us to find."

"How long does it take to make a fossil?" asks Milton.

"Sometimes not that long at all if conditions are right, but experts when they talk about fossils mean objects that are over 10,000 years old. The oldest fossils ever found are 3.5 billion years old but these are bacteria; simple lifeforms," answers Harriet.

Milton scratches his ear. "Is anything of the original object left?"

"Sometimes it disintegrates entirely, particularly if it is delicate like a fern," says Harriet. "What we dig up is the shape of where it was."

"An impression," says Milton, looking very pleased with himself.

"Exactly."

"And bones?" asks Milton.

"Bones are harder wearing than ferns. Their organic part – the softer material which makes up about 10 per cent – is usually replaced by minerals from the soil. The rest is the original bone itself gone through the petrifying process," replies Harriet.

"What about finding DNA in fossils like they do in the films?" Milton asks, excitedly. "Can we breed extinct creatures like dinosaurs?"

"That's very difficult as the DNA appears to have a 'best before' date," explains Harriet. "That means if it's kept too long it begins to degrade. Experts have found very old samples trapped in amber and in permafrost. They have also found it in bones and teeth. For example, they were able to extract DNA from a fossilized tooth from an extinct human species that's 110,000 years old, so who knows what we might be able to do in future? If it became possible to breed from such tiny traces, we would have to think hard before we woke up the creatures from the past."

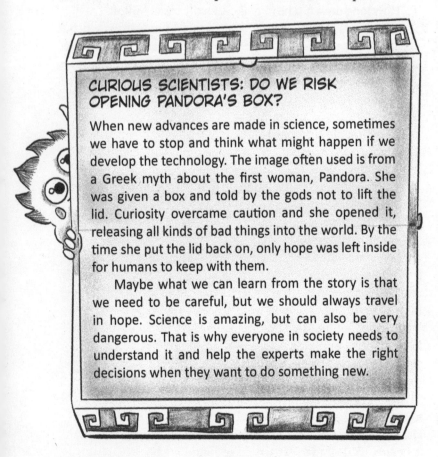

CURIOUS SCIENTISTS: DO WE RISK OPENING PANDORA'S BOX?

When new advances are made in science, sometimes we have to stop and think what might happen if we develop the technology. The image often used is from a Greek myth about the first woman, Pandora. She was given a box and told by the gods not to lift the lid. Curiosity overcame caution and she opened it, releasing all kinds of bad things into the world. By the time she put the lid back on, only hope was left inside for humans to keep with them.

Maybe what we can learn from the story is that we need to be careful, but we should always travel in hope. Science is amazing, but can also be very dangerous. That is why everyone in society needs to understand it and help the experts make the right decisions when they want to do something new.

The rock stars

"Do we only have the skull that got left in the taxi or are there other fossil examples of the southern apes?" asks Milton.

"Lots more have been found," says Harriet. "Let me introduce you to two of them – our rock stars."

Lucy

Lucy is a real rock star as she is named after the Beatles song "Lucy in the Sky with Diamonds" that was playing on the excavation when she was found in 1974. A team were digging in the Afar Depression of Ethiopia when they came across parts of the skeleton of a little female from around 3.2 million years ago. Only about 40 per cent survived but they could tell two important things: that she walked upright and that she had a small skull. That meant that these ancient creatures learned to walk before their brain size started to expand. This had been an intriguing puzzle as to which came first – big brain or walking on two feet.

Little Foot

Twenty years later, in 1994, Ronald J. Clarke was looking through a box of fossils from the Sterkfontein Cave in South Africa. He came across bones belonging to the left foot of a southern ape. In 1997, he led a team to the cave hoping to find more. What he did find was even better: the rest of the skeleton lying face down in the limestone. It was very hard to dig out of the rock so it took fifteen years of painstaking work to dig out an almost complete skeleton. Little Foot was harder to date than Lucy. The range is between 2.2–3.3 million years ago.

What did Little Foot tell us? Like Lucy he walked upright, but his opposable toe showed he was also adapted to live in trees as he could grasp branches (Lucy's feet hadn't survived). The feet are similar to a chimpanzee but the smaller hands are more like modern human hands.

MEET THE SCIENTISTS

LOUIS AND MARY LEAKEY

The most famous fossil hunting family of the twentieth century are the Leakeys.

LOUIS LEAKEY, FOSSIL HUNTING SPY

It started with Louis (1903–72) who grew up as the son of missionaries working in Kenya. He had an exciting childhood, and he learned the ways of the Kikuyu people and spoke their language. He was even initiated into the tribe in a secret ceremony that he was sworn never to speak of – and he never did!

As a teenager, he built a Kikuyu hut at the end of the garden for himself and moved in. It was there he kept his collection of natural history finds and dreamed of studying to become a scientist.

You passed... well done me!

When he went to university in Cambridge he mentioned to the authorities that he was fluent in Swahili. When it came to his final exam in this language he received two letters: one asking him to report for his examination; the other, with the same time and place, asking him to come to examine a candidate! Experts in Swahili were so rare that he had been asked to test himself by mistake. He also passed with honours in Kikuyu but because there was no one who spoke this language in the university, they accepted a certificate signed with a thumbprint from a Kikuyu chief saying Louis was fluent.

WANNA BET?

Louis returned to Africa to look for fossils showing human origins. His first major find was in the Olduvai Gorge in Tanzania. A German expert, Professor Hans Reck, had made some discoveries there that suggested human development went back much further than people thought at the time. Louis bet him ten pounds that he could dig for a day in the same gorge and find evidence to back up Reck's theory. Reck didn't think he would. Reck lost the bet because within twenty-four hours Louis had found ancient stone tools.

The name is Leakey, Louis Leakey.

During the Second World War, Louis worked as a spy, helping the colonial government deter enemy threats. His local knowledge came in very useful in unexpected ways. He helped an officer of the King's African Rifles remove a curse he had put on his men by mistake. Even during the war, he continued hunting for fossils on the sly.

MARY LEAKEY (1913-1996)

Mary was Louis's second wife and his colleague on many of his digs.

Mary first became interested in the story of human origins when at 12 she lived near Les Eyzies Cave in France. The archaeologist excavating the cave wasn't using modern methods and he threw out lots of things that would now be carefully examined. Mary got permission to go through his dump and found points, scrapers, and blades, which she began to put into groups, showing she had the instincts of a good archaeologist. Though she continued to volunteer on digs, she got into professional archaeology as an illustrator and met Louis when they worked on a book together. That was when her own career really took off. She found the first proconsul skull (another human ancestor) as well as many other specimens and tools. Proconsul, an extinct primate that lived 23–25 million years ago, was named after a popular chimpanzee on display at London zoo at the time of discovery.

Alas, poor primate!

WALKING WITH THE ANCESTORS

One of Mary's most exciting finds was the 3.7 million year old Laetoli footprints found in 1974. These are the marks of three ape-like creatures (possibly southern apes) walking upright, at a leisurely pace. Their feet are arched like modern humans, rather than flat-footed like a chimp. It's amazing they were preserved at all but they were rapidly filled with ash from a nearby volcano which is why they survived.

Louis and Mary's son, Richard (1944–), continued the fossil hunting tradition in the family, making many important finds. These included the Turkana Boy, an almost complete skeleton of a 12-year-old Homo ergaster or Homo erectus (scientists squabble about the name) which is 1.6 million years old. Richard turned to nature conservation but his wife Maeve and his daughter Louise continue the fossil research in Kenya.

"So what do the fossil finds tell us about modern humans?" asks Milton.

"The modern human species is called Homo sapiens," says Harriet. "Richard Leakey found fossils in Ethiopia dating from 195,000 years ago so they've been around at least that long."

Milton frowns. "Homo sapiens, Homo ergaster? Why do they have these odd names?"

"Science is an international joint effort," explains Harriet. "They try to name things so everyone can understand what they mean. Often they use Latin or Greek words to do this. It's not so hard when you see the pattern."

Harriet's Guide to Scientific Labels: What's in a name?

The scientific names for human ancestors can look difficult. In fact, once you see the pattern, they are much less daunting. Very often the name tells the story of where the fossil was found or something about what they were like.

• Australopithecus – southern ape – because they were apes and found first in southern Africa
• Homo habilis – handy man – because they had fingers giving precise grip
• Homo erectus – upright man – because they had long legs
• Homo ergaster – working man – because they used tools
• Homo neanderthalensis – Neanderthal man – because the fossils were first found in the Neander valley in Germany (Tal means "valley" in German)
• Homo heidelbergensis – Heidelberg man – because he was found in Heidelberg – get the pattern now?
• Homo sapiens – wise man – that's modern humans. They certainly can think, but are they also wise?
• Cro magnon man – a sub species of Homo sapiens found under a cliff locally known as Cro Magnon.
• So if you found a fossil of a new species in a back garden or school field, what would you call it? Homo goalpost-ensis, Homo wheelie-bins-ensis?

The dating game

"Other than digging up fossils, is there any other ways of telling how long humans have existed?" wonders Milton. "I mean, I know how old I am because I get a card on my birthday and candles on my cake."

"Experts use some special techniques to sort out the birthday cake and card," laughs Harriet. "To see how they do it, we need to follow a fossil from the dig where it was found to where the experts get to have a really good look at it. So it's back to the present for us and the place where we started: a laboratory."

Harriet sets the time machine into forward and rushes them to a big museum where experts are busy with a box of fossils.

Is it a match?

You can guess the age of an object by looking at the fossils and other materials found with it. For example, if you know another kind of animal like a sabre-toothed tiger was only found in the area at a certain time in prehistory, then you know roughly when that layer of rock was made. It's like a messy bedroom…

I told you to tidy your bedroom last week.

But I did!

No you didn't. I can see your smelly tennis socks from the match last Tuesday.

Rumbled.

Dating app

Another tool the experts can use are machines that can do something called radiometric dating. They use natural radioactivity – this is the safe, ordinary sort that is found in everything from bananas to boulders. As time passes, some radioactive materials change in a way that can be reliably tracked, like the countdown on a clock. If the fossil comes from an area that had volcanoes the experts look for an element called potassium. An unstable part of that (called an isotope) changes over time to a gas called argon.

Using this method, the base of the Olduvai Gorge, where the Leakeys worked and found many fossils, has been dated to 1.9 million years old.

The second technique is something you've probably already heard about: carbon dating. An unstable form of the element carbon (carbon-14) is produced all the time in the atmosphere thanks to cosmic radiation. Living things then take it into their bodies while they are alive but stop when they die. Carbon-14 then breaks down by radioactive decay at a reliable rate so you can look at how much is left in a sample and estimate how long it was since the creature or plant died. This clock has a limit before the carbon-14 trace is too small to measure. Scientists think it can only be used to date objects reliably from the last 40,000 years.

Dating game, set, and match!

Experts have a new tool to use: DNA. There are three types to look for:

Mr Junk Info

You know those instruction manuals that come in many languages? You only read a few pages and ignore the rest? Nuclear DNA that we inherit from both parents is like that – full of junk information that doesn't get used. It still gets passed on to each generation. Scientists can follow how this changes over time and work out ancestral relationships. Looking at this, they have found great variation in the African populations and less in the rest of the world. This has led scientists to think that the people who established non-African populations left the continent about 90,000 years ago. The rest of the world is descended from a smaller group than those who stayed behind in Africa.

Why Man

Humans have either XX (female) or XY (male) chromosomes. Parents send one chromosome deciding gender to the embryo. The Y chromosome comes from the male side, but there's a 50 per cent chance the male might send an X which is why we have roughly equal numbers of males and females born.

Experts have looked for changes in the Y chromosome in DNA and found it doesn't change very much. The little mutations they have detected suggest the original male of the Homo sapiens may have lived around 150,000 years ago in Africa. They have dubbed this ancestor "Adam" after the first man in the Bible. They don't mean that he is the same as Adam, just that is how far back they can trace the Y chromosome journey.

Mighty Mama

The last kind of DNA is found in part of a human cell outside the nucleus, the mitochondria. This is only inherited from the mother. This is easier to track than the Y chromosome information and scientists have dated a common female ancestor to modern humans about 200,000 to 150,000 years ago in Africa. And yes, they called her "Mitochondrial Eve" after the first woman in the Bible.

The great bottleneck

Both the Y Adam and Mitochondrial Eve evidence hints that the human population passed through a bottleneck at some point in prehistory. How do we know this? Our closest relations among living ape species show big variations in these DNA inheritances compared to us. It's something of a mystery but evidence suggests the human population dropped to very low numbers at one point, maybe due to a crisis or change in the environment. When numbers recovered, there was a smaller number to pass on less varied DNA to future generations.

This is one of those areas where science is still discovering new things with lots more work for future experts. What do you think might have happened? How might we find out the answers?

African cradle for curiosity

Milton looks very pleased with himself. "I think I'm getting the hang of this. Homo sapiens, or modern humans, started in Africa and spread out to the rest of the planet. Then they started having complex thoughts, and painting pictures."

Harriet shakes her head, slowly. "Um, no. That's what I was trying to tell you. We find pictures everywhere so it is likely that the first humans took the idea of using symbols to describe their place in the world with them. Otherwise people everywhere would've had to invent it on their own and that's much less probable. Though not all scientists agree on this."

Milton gets a bit grumpy to have his ideas knocked down. "Go on then, prove it."

Harriet isn't annoyed with him but pleased with the challenge. "Ooh, that's a good scientific question! But it's really hard to do because many of their works only survive by fluke."

"Ah, so you can't prove it?" Milton flicks his tail.

"I can try. Let me show you something from Sulawesi – that's in Indonesia." She calls up a picture of pig deer surrounded by handprints on the view screen on the time machine controls.

"Hey, that's like some of the pictures we saw in France!" exclaims Milton.

Harriet nods. "Yes, but even a little older, some 40,000 years old. Scientists had thought European humans led the way in cave paintings, but others were actually at it too! Either both groups thought up making pictures on their own or they already knew about it.

"But to cast more light on this, I can show you the earliest known engravings," continues Harriet. "For that we need to go on an archaeological dig in the Blombos Cave, South Africa, in 2002. They are about to dig up what might be the earliest example of abstract art from around 77,000 years ago."

BLOMBOS CAVE

YEAH!

When first made, this ochre would have been the colour of blood.

Harriet and Milton get back in the time machine.

"And the mind-blowing thing, Milton, is that maybe modern humans weren't the first. Archaeologists found something amazing in 2014 in East Java. Scientists came across a shell that someone had doodled on with zigzags. They dated it to 430,000 years ago."

Milton interrupts washing his paws. "Hang on a minute! I thought modern humans were only around 260,000 years old!"

"Exactly, it was done by an ancestor, now extinct, called Homo erectus."

"I remember that one – upright man with the long legs. Wow. So the idea of drawing and making signs has been around for a long, long time!" says Milton, excitedly.

"Scientists wonder if the idea isn't somehow embedded in the human brain, something that goes along with advances in tool technology and movement to new and challenging environments. Something that goes along with asking questions," says Harriet.

Milton frowns. "Or maybe Mr Homo erectus was just doodling and it didn't mean anything?"

"Maybe," replies Harriet, "but he was using a pointed stylus and doing something with it intentionally. What other patterns might he and others in his community have left elsewhere? We've found one; maybe there are more out there for new explorers to discover?"

Getting burials rite (warning: not for the squeamish!)

Harriet is enjoying rising to Milton's challenge to the idea that Africa was the cradle of curiosity. "You asked me to prove that humans carried out of Africa complex thoughts about their place in the world, so I've one final piece of evidence I'd like to show you. But you've got to be up for a bit of skull handling."

"Nothing I like better," says Milton, not very truthfully. He is a scaredy-cat sometimes.

Harriet sets the destination for the Herto caves in eastern Ethiopia. "The oldest ritual burial we have found so far is in Israel at a place called Es Skhul on Mount Carmel. The bodies look like they were buried with jewellery made of shells."

"Shell necklaces – like the Red not-a-Lady of Paviland?" asks Milton.

"Exactly," says Harriet. "That burial in Israel is about 90,000 years old. But the one in Herto is far older."

They get out of the time machine and find themselves in the middle of another archaeological dig.

"What are they doing?" whispers Milton.

"They've found two adult skulls and one child but the child one is smashed to bits," Harriet whispers back.

Milton looks a bit queasy. "So they are doing a skull puzzle?"

"Yes. And here's the grisly bit," Harriet says. "From the cut marks, it looks like the flesh was taken off the skulls first and they've been rubbed smooth. Hair, skin, everything taken off on purpose and not because they were going to be eaten for dinner."

Milton keels over so Harriet splashes water on his face to wake him up.

"Come on, Milton: we think they meant it nicely," Harriet chuckles. "Perhaps a sign of respect or death ritual?"

"Very respectful," says Milton grimly. "I'm keeping my skin on, thanks!"

Neanderthals were doing it too

"Are you ready for another burial?" asks Harriet gently.

Milton looks a little squeamish. "If we must."

"It's just that modern humans aren't the only ones who had elaborate burial rites," explains Harriet. "The Neanderthals did too."

Milton remembers the family tree she showed him. "Those are the ones named after the Neander Valley in Germany?"

"That's right, but they were spread all over Europe and parts of Asia," says Harriet.

"What were they like?" asks Milton.

81

"It seems that they lived alongside modern humans for at least 5,000 years," replies Harriet, "and a few had offspring together as the human genome shows 1–4 per cent Neanderthal in the genes."

WHAT IS THE HUMAN GENOME?

This is a complete set of all the human genes. It is a bit like a massive recipe book of how to make a human. The first scientific map of the human genome was completed in 2003. Neanderthals also got their own recipe book, first mapped in 2009, which is how we know the two species mixed with each other.

"Evidence isn't strong," Harriet continues, "but it seems they may have intentionally buried their dead and also been cave painters. But scientists have a long way to go before they can all agree on this."

PRIMATE PARALLELS

Milton has now recovered from skull handling and is eager to get on with the quest. "So it's clear that humans are pretty special: making things, coming up with statues and pictures and tools so long ago."

"That's right," Harriet agrees. "But have you ever wondered just how special? What makes them different from other apes? If you went by just the technical description of what makes an ape then there's not much difference."

WHAT'S IN AN APE?

Biologists define an ape as having:
- an appendix
- an adapted elbow joint – this is so they can rotate their hands easily (try it now!)
- but no tail (pity!)

"Their closest relation in the animal kingdom is the chimpanzee," Harriet tells Milton.

Where do humans fit in the family tree?

"Remember the fossil hunting spy, Louis Leakey?" asks Harriet. "He was one of the people to find fossils for the most famous of the ancestral apes, Proconsul, in the decades after the Second World War. Looking at the human family tree, Louis began asking the same questions as us: just how different were humans to other apes? He took a surprising next step."

Milton pauses in licking his paw. "What's that?"

"Over the next few decades, he persuaded three colleagues to set up research into living apes, not fossil ones. The names of the researchers were Jane Goodall, Dian Fossey, and Biruté Galdikas. They were called Leakey's Angels after a TV show of the time, starring a team of female detectives.

"Three animal-loving detectives! I'd like to go and visit them," says Milton.

Harriet inputs the coordinates for Africa. "We'll go to the chimps first, as they are the closest to humans."

Jane Goodall and the chimpanzees

Harriet and Milton get out of the time machine in the Gombe Stream National Park in Tanzania. The date is 1960, when the young scientist has just begun her study of the chimps living in the park. She's given them names to help identify them, such as David Greybeard and Fifi.

They form friendships.

They hold hands and embrace when upset.

They have different ways of greeting different members of the community.

Scientists once thought that humans were the only tool-makers, but these chimps make tools by carefully removing leaves from stems to get termites (or ants) out of their nests to eat.

So we must now redefine tools, or accept chimpanzees as human!

Once you look for tool use among animals, you find it everywhere. Here's a list of Milton's favourite handy creatures… and not all of them have hands!

MILTON'S LIST OF THE TOP TEN TOOL-USING ANIMALS WHO AREN'T APES

• Crows: the first animal tool user to be spotted by a human – the Ancient Greek storyteller Aesop who wrote a fable about it. These clever birds drop stones in containers to raise the water level so they can drink. They use a variety of tools and make their own toys.

• Dolphins: a safety conscious community of dolphins in Shark Bay, Australia, carry sea sponges on their noses for protection when rooting in the sandy seabed for food. Some have also been seen using conch shells to scoop up prey and carry them to the surface to eat.

I've a nose for trouble.

• Sea otters: these handy creatures use stones to crack open the hard shells of prey or dislodge them from rocks. They even have a special loose pouch of skin across their chests in which they carry their stone which is their version of a tool belt.

- Elephants: they have been seen to use a variety of tools, including one that shows great forward planning. They drop rocks into a waterhole to plug it so the water doesn't evaporate and is there when they want to drink later in the dry season.
- Finch woodpeckers: these clever birds use sticks to get at larvae when their beak isn't quite long enough.
- Capuchin monkeys: these natural lollipop eaters have been seen to poke a twig into a source of sticky food and lick!
- Macaques: these monkeys are one of the most inventive creatures. One group at a Buddhist shrine in Thailand has learned to pluck out hair from unwary visitors to use as dental floss. Mothers even slow down their actions to show their babies how to floss properly.

That was a hair-raising visit!

- Mandrills: on a similar theme, some mandrills have been seen using sticks to clean their ears.
- Egyptian vultures: they have learned how to crack an egg. They pick up stones and throw them at the egg

until it breaks, apparently preferring rounded stones rather than sharp ones for the job.

• Octopuses: one species has been seen making portable armour out of discarded coconut shells. It then returns sometimes to the coconut pile to use it as a shelter. They have also been seen to build fences out of stones and shells.

While Jane Goodall writes up her observations from that morning, Milton and Harriet discuss his list of animal tool users. Milton is very happy with it as he feels it has changed the way he thinks about other animals.

"This proves, doesn't it, Harriet, that using tools is fairly common in the animal kingdom?"

"Yes. But it also raises a curious question." Harriet pins the list up next to the chart of human origins. "If other animals act like humans, experimenting with tools to find the one to fit the task, does that mean they see the world in the same way too?"

"How can we ever know what someone else is thinking?" muses Milton.

"You could try this experiment. It's the standard one used by experts."

TRY THIS AT HOME!

Put a dab of rouge on the forehead of the test subject (though it can be anything harmless, like a little sticker that stands out from their skin colour), wait a while, then show the animal their face in a mirror. If the test subject explores the sticker on its own forehead, this is taken as a sign that they have the ability of self recognition (meaning they know it is them in the mirror, not another animal). Normally, human babies pass the test, but other animals, like dogs, don't.

- ☑ Great apes (including humans)
- ☑ Dolphins and orcas
- ☑ Eurasian magpie
- ☒ Several monkey species
- ☒ Dogs
- ☒ Pandas
- ☒ Sea lions

Using a little sticker, you could try this on a family pet if you have one – but obviously not the goldfish, please![2] Does your cat recognize itself? Does your dog bark at the mirror as if it is a rival or ignore it? What does your hamster think of its reflection?

Do you think this is a good experiment? What species would you like to test it out on if you could?

---

[2] Scientists also have to learn how to do their research safely and responsibly. Always ask permission from an adult before trying an experiment and explain exactly what you are going to do.

WASHOE: THE CLEVER CHIMP (1965-2007)

Chimps in the wild have many clever ways of dealing with their environment, but in captivity some have proved to be extraordinary. Washoe was captured from the wild in West Africa by the US airforce with the idea that she might be part of the space programme. Instead, she was taken into the home of two scientists from the University of Nevada, Allen and Beatrix Gardner, and raised very much like a human child. She wore clothes and sat with them at the dinner table. They taught her American Sign Language (ASL) and she learned around 350 words.

When she was five, the Gardners decided to move on to another project and she was sent to the Oklahoma Institute of Primate Studies. At first, she was shocked to be among other chimps and to learn that she wasn't human. She carried on communicating through ASL with the researchers, showing amazing abilities, passing the rouge test, and making particular friendships with the researchers. Later, she taught some of the signs to her adopted chimp son, Loulis.

Washoe's case is very exciting but it also raises some challenging questions. Was it right to treat her this way, making her live like a human child then suddenly putting her among her own kind? What rights should Washoe have had as she was self-aware and able to talk in signs and form friendships with humans? This question is now being explored in law on behalf of other great apes.

Do chimps feel awe and wonder?

In the afternoon, Harriet and Milton go with Jane to look for more chimps to watch.

"One of the most interesting puzzles for us human observers," explains Jane, "is working out what chimps are feeling. Sometimes they do things that look very like our own ways of behaving. For example, they show signs of feeling awe and wonder."

"Really?" asks Milton, not at all sure about that. "How can you know?"

"Come and see the waterfall dance," Jane smiles.

Jane takes Harriet and Milton to an impressive waterfall and they lie in wait for a party of seven young male chimps. This is what happens…

Chimps and the Waterfall Dance

They set out to explore...

...and find a waterfall.

They decide who is going to go first...

... to swing out over the water. Others just sit
and enjoy the view.

"It's amazing, isn't it?" whispers Harriet to Milton. "They do this during a heavy rainstorm too. Jane thinks chimpanzees are as spiritual as we are but it is locked up inside them. This dance is how they express it."[3]

Leaf loo paper

After thanking Jane for her time, Harriet and Milton get back into the time machine, very impressed by the waterfall dance.

"So if chimps can feel awe at nature, does that mean they are religious?" asks Milton.

"That's a difficult question," says Harriet. "Religion can just mean performing rituals, and chimps seem to do that. Jane told us that she thinks they are spiritual, and that is about what is going on inside them which is hard to know for certain. Recently, a scientist found a group of chimpanzees in West Africa building a stone heap (called a cairn) at the foot of a scarred tree for no apparent reason. Some have speculated that it is a kind of altar, but that is maybe going a step too far. Some think that the stone cairn building does continue to close the gap between human and chimp behaviour.

"There's something else that's funny about chimps. They also have different technological traditions depending where they live. Take, for example, the tricky question of leaf loo paper!"

"Leaf loo paper?" Milton looks a little disgusted by the idea. "What's wrong with washing your bum with your tongue?"

"That's what all cats do, but chimps have other ideas on the subject," explains Harriet. "Here, take a look at this report from two chimp reserves, the one we've just visited in Tanzania, and another in the Tai forest of West Africa, thousands of miles away. What's normal for one is a mystery to the other."

---

3 Watch this great YouTube video of the chimps: https://www.youtube.com/watch?v=jjQCZClpaaY

"So chimps have dreamed up tools in different parts of Africa but, because they've not been in contact with each other, these ideas haven't spread?" asks Milton.

"That's what it looks like," agrees Harriet. "I came across something similar with bears in America. The ones in Yosemite National Park in California have become really good at getting to campers' food, even breaking into cars to get at picnics. The ones in Yellowstone National Park hundred of miles away don't do this – at least, not yet!"

"I didn't like to mention it to her today in what was 1960," says Harriet, "but Jane went on to find out that chimps also feel much more dangerous emotions than awe and wonder. In the mid-1970s, one of the chimp groups split into two sets of rival males and went to war. Sadly that ended with the killing of male rivals and some of the females. This was the first time she had seen chimps deliberately kill each other. The war lasted for four years but most of the territorial gains made by one group getting rid of the other were quickly lost to yet another stronger group."

"That's depressing," says Milton. "So the chimp-on-chimp murder was for nothing?"

Harriet looks sad. "Yes, but they didn't know that then, did they? Perhaps it's time we visit a different ape society – the mountain gorillas – and see how they manage their relationships."

"Not another war, I hope?" says Milton.

Grumpy gorillas

"So for our next visit on the great ape trail, we're off to visit Dian Fossey's gorillas in Rwanda in Africa in our present day," says Harriet. "These mountain gorillas are an endangered species with only about 880 left. They need looking after, not only because they can teach us a lot about how apes think, but because they are wonderful creatures."

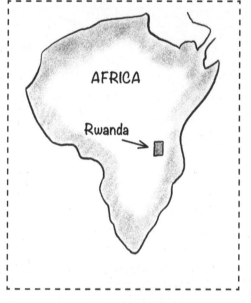

"It would be terrible if we could only visit them with a time machine," frets Milton. "People need to see them in the flesh and not just on video taken in the past."

"That's right but, unfortunately, there is a big problem with poachers who kill them for trophies," says Harriet, sadly. "They do stupid things like cutting off their hands to sell as ash trays. Dian Fossey herself was killed in 1985. Her murder was never solved and some people wonder if it was the work of poachers who didn't want her to get in their way. It also reminds us how brave some scientists have to be to do their job."

The box lands with a thump in the middle of a mountain forest. Our intrepid time travellers get out to find themselves surrounded by mist.

"Let's go quietly... we don't want to come across them unexpectedly," whispers Harriet.

 **AARGH!**

"Back away, slowly," Milton says. "That's normal speed for you, Harriet."

"Don't worry, I don't think he's that interested in us. You see, there's an intriguing side to these creatures," explains Harriet. "They spend most of their time worrying about each other. Scientists worked this out because, although gorillas have a big brain, they seem less clever at solving puzzles in the wild than in captivity."

Milton frowns. "What kind of clever?" he asks.

"That's a great question! It's not that they are dumb in the wild, but it looks like their minds are on other things than puzzles in their natural surroundings."

"What kind of things?"

"Well, it's just like school really…"

Harriet and Milton crouch down in the undergrowth to watch the great silverback gorilla sit in the middle of his family.

"Just like humans," whispers Harriet, "it seems that much of the gorilla brain is focused on working out where he or she fits in her family, how to make friends, and deal with arguments. That doesn't leave time for much else."

Milton thinks for a moment. "So maybe that's why humans developed large brains as well – they had to have a lot of space to think about their relationships?"

"Scientists think you might be right. Let's have a look at how other apes organize themselves," suggests Harriet.

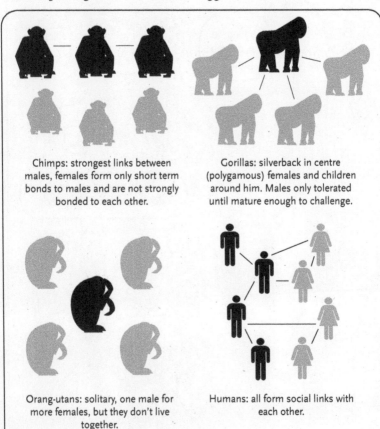

Chimps: strongest links between males, females form only short term bonds to males and are not strongly bonded to each other.

Gorillas: silverback in centre (polygamous) females and children around him. Males only tolerated until mature enough to challenge.

Orang-utans: solitary, one male for more females, but they don't live together.

Humans: all form social links with each other.

Orang-utans: exceptional apes

I want to be alone.

"Looking at that chart, it seems that the orang-utans are the odd one out among the great apes," says Milton. "They have big ape brains that should be full of social ideas but instead they like to live alone."

"Yes, it is odd," agrees Harriet, entering the coordinates in the time machine computer. "I think we should go and visit one."

"But they don't like visitors," warns Milton.

Harriet smiles. "We'll be careful. We only have two choices: orang-utans are found either in the rainforests of Borneo or Sumatra."

"Where does the last of Leakey's Angels work?" asks Milton.

"Biruté Galdikas studies the orang-utans of Borneo."

"Right," says Milton, curling up in his chair ready for take off. "That's where we're going."

The world flicks by the porthole and the two explorers arrive in the steamy jungles of Borneo.

"I've been looking up orang-utan while we were on the way," says Milton.

Harriet is very impressed at Milton doing his own research. "And what did you find out?"

He shows her his notes.

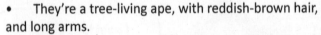

MILTON'S NOTES ON ORANG-UTANS

- They're a tree-living ape, with reddish-brown hair, and long arms.
- Their hands are very like human ones, but they have opposable toes which means they can hold things with their feet.
- The males tend to be much bigger than the females and some of the biggest males even grow moustaches!
- They live in loosely bonded groups where they spend most of their time alone, except for the mothers and children.
- The mothers have babies about once every eight years which is one of the biggest gaps in the animal kingdom, but gives the mother time to raise the children.
- Their name means "person of the forest" in Malay.
- They use tools and build bed-nests each night.
- They might have technological traditions like the chimps do, but that is still being studied.
- They are under threat of extinction, with only about 60,000 left.

Milton and Harriet find one of Biruté Galdikas's research team watching as an orang-utan prepares her bed for the night in the treetop. The orang-utan baby is looking on, studying how she does it. The mother carefully braids the branches together to form a platform, then adds leaves to make herself pillows and blankets.

While Milton and Harriet are admiring the orang-utan's skill at nesting, smoke rises in the distance.

"Sorry for interrupting, but what's causing the fire?" Milton asks the researcher.

"That's a logging party, clearing the rainforest to grow palm oil," she explains. "It's used in many products you can buy all over the world, from cosmetics to fuel. The biggest threat to the great apes around the world comes from people destroying the places they live. If we want these wonderful creatures to avoid extinction, we have to protect the rainforests and stop companies doing this.

"Another threat is from poachers," the researcher continues, sadly, "and people catching orang-utans to make them into pets, killing the mothers to take the babies while they are cute. Once they reach adulthood, the orang-utans are too big and too clever to be kept that way, so are often abandoned. We have a community of rescued orang-utans that Biruté Galdikas's foundation looks after but it would be better of course if they didn't have to be saved in the first place."

The researcher scratches Milton softly behind the ear. "All of us have a part to play in protecting the apes by what we choose to buy and what we ask our political leaders to do for the environment."

HORIZONS OF CURIOSITY

Saddened by seeing the rainforest destroyed, Milton and Harriet get back into the time machine.

"This doesn't run on palm oil does it?" asks Milton, sniffing the engine.

"No, fortunately not." Harriet taps the control desk. "It runs on an advanced form of energy that will be invented in the future. But it is a good question for here and now. We can sometimes think we don't have anything to do with problems on the other side of the world, when we are actually helping create them. We do that when we buy things that have ingredients grown where there used to be rainforest."

"So what have we learnt from the great apes?" asks Milton, settling back in his chair.

"You tell me, Milton. You've become quite the ape expert."

Pleased to be asked, Milton produces his first scientific paper.

MILTON'S BEST GUESSES: APES

- In many ways, humans are very like apes, and not just because they have no tail, an appendix, and an adapted elbow joint.
- Chimps share 98 per cent of the same genetic material.
- Human researchers recognize behaviours in other apes that we think of as human, including offering friendship and comfort, as well as making war.

- Chimps show signs of spiritual response to the world around them.
- Many apes use tools and build structures, inventing a basic technology that is shared by certain populations and not others.
- They spend a lot of time worrying about social relationships in their group and this takes up a lot of brain power and possibly explains the brain's large size.

Conclusion: Other apes aren't so different from humans but something happened to make humans take some of these skills (tool usage, social interaction, spiritual response) and go a lot further with them.

"So far, we just seem to be finding out that humans are very like other creatures but there must be something else we haven't noticed that made them go further with tools, artworks, awe, and wonder," muses Milton. "Chimpanzees haven't painted portraits or written books. Gorillas haven't built cities or journeyed to the moon."

Harriet munches thoughtfully on a lettuce leaf. "I think it is all to do with the human super power."

Milton falls off his chair in excitement. "What super power?"

"We've been talking about it already," Harriet laughs. "One of the things which separates humans from other creatures is curiosity. All animals are curious, but humans have no limits on the questions they want answering. Think of it like this. Even simple life forms, like bacteria, find out about the world by bumping into other simple creatures. That's how they explore. Moving up a level, complex creatures use a wide variety of senses to find out what's around them, what they can eat, what is a threat. It's all part of testing their horizons. Humans do that too, but they also look behind the answer for the cause in a way few other creatures do."

TRY THIS AT HOME:
HOW LONG IS A PIECE OF STRING?

Here's an experiment to test if a creature has the kind of curiosity which will encourage them to look and see what is causing an action. You will need:

- an obliging cat
- a baby, preferably sitting in a high chair (please first ask permission from the parent and make sure the baby is safe at all times)

Take a piece of string or a toy and dangle it in front of the test subject. Move it and see what they do. The cat will probably have hours of fun chasing the string, never once wondering what is causing the movement. A baby is likely to get bored more easily and will quickly look to you as the source of the string or toy movement. She might laugh, and share the joke with you. She understands that you are behind the test in the way a cat does not appear to.

Is this what you saw when you tried this? Did you get a different reaction from other animals you did the experiment with?

"The big thing is," says Harriet, "that curiosity loses its horizon when we can talk and ask questions. That's maybe why humans have gone so much further than other animals with their thinking about art, science, and religion.

"Washoe the chimp learned quite a few words but she was only able to combine them in a limited way. She didn't ask the most powerful question of all, one that most little children learn very early on."

"What?" asks Milton excitedly.

"No. The most powerful question is…"

"What is it?"

"No, I already said it isn't 'what,'" explains Harriet.

"No," says Milton, impatiently, "I'm not saying the question is 'what'; I'm asking what the question is."

"Then I'll tell you the answer. The most powerful question in the world is…"

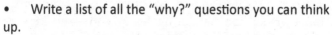

TRY THIS AT HOME: THE NEVER-ENDING QUESTIONS

• Write a list of all the "why?" questions you can think up.

• Now group them into sets that invite different kinds of answers. Examples might be i) moral – "why is it wrong to steal?" ii) social – "why doesn't she like me?" iii) scientific – "why is the sky blue?" iv) spiritual – "why does the universe exist?"

Humans have been asking questions like this for centuries. The attempt to find an answer lies at the root of all of our cultures, science, and faith. Some of these questions deal with the ultimate things in life – the meaning and purpose of why we are here – and some deal with other matters; things which could be called "penultimate questions". Very often the two run together because asking a scientific questions such as "why is the universe how it is?" might also lead to the question of why is there a universe at all?

Challenge: try and come up with a scientific "why?" question that has not been answered yet.

WHAT DOES PENULTIMATE MEAN?

• "Ultimate" in Latin means "last" and "paene" means "almost" so joined together they mean "almost last" or "next to last".

Caught not taught

"So humans are the creatures that ask 'why?'" summarizes Milton.

"Yes," confirms Harriet. "And because they use language to communicate, they are also able to pass on both questions and answers."

Milton looks puzzled. "How does that help?"

"Remember the stone tool-using chimps of the Tai Forest?" asks Harriet. "The researchers watching their community for over fifty years noticed that during that time the skills were more caught than taught. Occasionally, mother chimps would stop and show the young ones how to do things, but mostly the children just watched and picked it up. They were catching on to ideas, not being carefully instructed.

"Another thing the scientists noticed was that there was no technological progress during all the time the chimps were under observation," explains Harriet. "No one made a better stone tool; they were stuck at the same level. That separates chimps from humans. People can talk about their tools, ask questions about how to make them better, and experiment. This strategy means they can keep on making improvements and inventing new things."

Welcome to the cathedral of the mind

Milton finds this very exciting. "So curiosity is the human super power and makes them ask super questions? But why them? Why not chimps?"

Harriet thinks for a moment. "I'm not sure. I've been leading this quest, but you've had some excellent ideas too. What do you think?"

Milton is flattered she thinks he has any interesting notions at all. He licks his hind leg for a moment before one comes to him.

"I know! Maybe their brains are organized differently? I heard a scientist once say that you could think of the mind like a big cathedral, full of different areas and side chapels. If you think of a chimp's brain, what do you imagine is going on inside? I'll show you my idea.

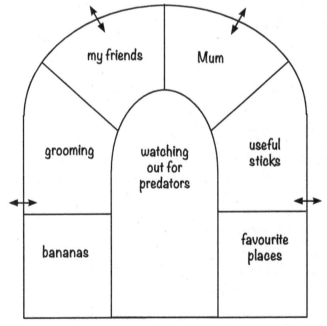

"My theory is that chimps don't join up all these thoughts but tend to keep to established patterns. It's like he goes through a separate entrance to access each one," says Milton. "Let's think how a human brain might look if it were imagined as a cathedral."

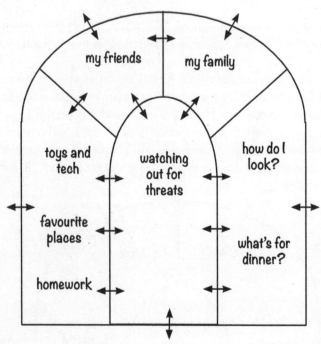

"I think the human brain has knocked through all the different side chapels and created many new pathways so that thinking can circulate between ideas," concludes Milton. "There's even a special name for this."

"What is it?" asks Harriet.

Special name for special thinking:
Cognitive fluidity... or SLIPPERY THINKING!

"And what's really brilliant, Milton," says Harriet, giving him a pat on the back, "is that you've showed slippery thinking by linking up what you'd once heard a scientist say with what we are talking about today. So humans, and we two exceptional time travellers, are all slippery thinkers. That might be the very thing that has made humans different from other apes."

Milton takes a moment to preen.

"I have another question for you," says Harriet.

"Sock it to me," says Milton, feeling ready for anything.

"We've visited lots of humans and their ancestors. Who was the first slippery thinker?" ponders Harriet.

"Oh." Milton isn't sure.

"The cave painters?" Harriet muses.

"Clearly they were doing slippery thinking already as they were using signs, so yes. It's them," concludes Milton.

Harriet smiles. "What about the Neanderthals and the signs we saw that they made special burials, buildings, and possibly cave paintings too?"

Milton frowns. "Um…"

"And then there was the zigzag shell doodle of the Homo erectus ancestor from half a million years ago," says Harriet.

Milton recalls what he has learned on his journey. "I know, Harriet, I don't have a 'for sure' answer but I have a best guess!"

"Tell me your best guess, Milton," says Harriet.

"We can't put a start date on curiosity," Milton says, "because we are unlikely to have a fossil or find that proves it. What survives is just luck and chance conditions."

"Good…" Harriet encourages.

"But we can say if we see signs of ancestors using symbols, which suggest a slippery kind of thought process connecting things up, that curiosity must've started *before* a certain date. So I'd say it was at least half a million years old and I'd expect it to go much further back," states Milton.

"I agree," nods Harriet.

"So curiosity is curiously old." He purrs at his conclusion as Harriet applauds his theory.

HOW DO WE KNOW RIGHT FROM WRONG?

Their box is spinning through time and space. Harriet has set a new destination; she won't tell Milton where they are going but asks him to guess.

"Right, so we've looked at how humans learn differently from other apes, how they join up their thinking, and use symbols like language and pictures. So are you taking me to see something new?" Milton asks.

"Yes," says Harriet. "If I were to ask you what is very different about humans, what would you say?"

"They make fart jokes?" Milton wonders.

"There is that," Harriet laughs, "but I was thinking of something more basic."

Milton can only think about jokes now. "You're going to have to tell me."

"Nearly everyone everywhere has a well-developed sense of right and wrong, a moral sense if you like," explains Harriet. "That isn't the same as what they then go on to do, but humans are used to their actions and the actions of others being held up against standards that most in their society share, such as it is wrong to hurt others, or to steal."

Milton nods. "OK, I see that. So where does this moral sense come from? We saw there were hints that chimps felt awe and wonder. What about knowing right and wrong?"

"Again, it is almost impossible to judge what's going on inside another animal's head," says Harriet. "One thing we can look at though is how willing they are to act against their own self interest as other bonds overrule it.

"Compare swallows with deer. My master, Charles Darwin,

noted that if swallows had a brood late on in the season, they didn't seem to fret when the migratory instinct kicked in. They would abandon the nest and young ones without looking back, leaving for warmer climates in the interests of their own survival. With migrating deer, we see something very different. When the herd is moving, the mothers go back and check on the young ones who might be lagging behind or having trouble keeping up with the adults. They risk their own survival if separated from the herd to encourage their offspring."

"It's tricky to make simple deductions from this," continues Harriet, "but this might be the beginnings of a moral sense. Maybe the mother deer can imagine the pain of being left behind so tries to prevent it. Imagining what it would feel like to be in another's situation is arguably the start of thinking how your actions affect others and the basis on which we all decide what's right and what's wrong."

"So where are we going?" asks Milton, seeing some buildings and an ice cream kiosk outside the porthole. "Did you decide you knew how much I wanted an ice cream and that it would be the right thing to do to bring me here?"

Harriet rolls her eyes. "That's not the right and wrong I'm talking about. No, I've brought you to see the chimp community kept in Arnhem zoo in 1975. Keeping a close eye on what the chimps do every day, the researchers have noticed they help others in their group even when it's not in their own self-interest. These young chimps know to help the aged."

"These look like friendly chimps," agrees Milton, licking the sardine-flavoured ice cream Harriet has bought him, "but I can't forget the sad story about the four year war in the Gombe reservation. If these chimps know to help an elderly one, why didn't those warrior apes stop before they started killing each other and innocent females?"

"Well, that's the question, isn't it?" says Harriet. "You can ask the same thing of so many human societies. I'd say that the chimps in Gombe at least didn't have more complex ideas about what society they were trying to create; they weren't able to stand outside their situation and look at it without bias. That makes them less at fault. Humans know all this but still they fight.

"Yet at least the emergence of a moral sense in some apes gives us a rule to say when something is right and something is wrong. You can't say that about swallows; they can't defeat their survival instinct."

"Grim news for the poor fledglings." Milton then tries to cheer them up with a joke. "Harriet, when is an ape fight not a chimpanzee battle?"

"I don't know, Milton," sighs Harriet. "When is an ape fight not a chimpanzee battle?"

"When its gorilla[4] warfare!" He beams.

Harriet nudges him. "I'm happy you came along with me on our quest."

Milton looks very pleased. "That's what friends are for."

"There's one more idea I want to introduce you to before we go back to your master's study," says Harriet.

Milton finishes his ice cream. "I'm ready."

"It's a biggie," Harriet warns.

Milton puffs up his fur. "I'm still ready. Tell me what it is."

"It's freedom."

---

[4] Guerrilla

Harriet's Big Idea:
What do we mean by freedom?

If human brains are only a development of other animals' way of thinking, how can humans believe themselves to be free to act and make choices? Why aren't humans just like the swallows, driven by survival instincts for which they can't be blamed?

You can argue this but if you go down this route, then responsibility for actions disappears as an idea. There would be no right or wrong, just as we don't blame swallows for giving in to the urge to fly away.

However, the human brain is different. Thanks to the cathedral of the mind, humans are able to consider their own thoughts as a whole and take an overview of the consequences of their choices and actions. They can look at the big picture.

"Mary Midgley was a famous philosopher," said Harriet, "and she said that this ability to connect things up was what gives humans their freedom and that it wasn't just an illusion, but something real. Humans can look at the thoughts of their own minds and set priorities. Talking to others, they can agree on lasting principles and rules (morals and laws). For example, humans don't have to commit murder and find out from the consequences that it was bad; they can imagine and discuss with others what might happen and then agree."

Thou shalt not kill.

"And another thing," continued Harriet, "for this to hold true for you from one moment to the next, you have to have the overarching idea that your reality is one in which 'you' exist, that you are the same person today as yesterday. If this wasn't the case then how could you be responsible for something that was done by that past 'you'?"

"I'm confused," said Milton, puzzled.

"Try this! Think of your own idea of yourself like a constant in your mind, equivalent to the magnetic north on a compass. If you keep checking with that, you'll find your way through life and the choices you are free to make will keep to a consistent course.

"In summary, for a human to act as a whole, they have to have a big picture into which they can fit things."

"Our journey is all about how science fits into the big picture," said Milton, excitedly.

Four heads are better than one

Harriet sets the dial in the time machine.

"I'm taking you back to the cave where we started," she says.

"Why are you doing that?" wonders Milton.

"Well, now we've been on this journey, I want to look at the

Chauvet paintings again," says Harriet. "I want us to look very closely at just two of them."

"I'm happy to do that," says Milton, happily. "I've learned so much about people on this journey and I'd enjoy seeing the cave people in action again."

"You'll have to keep quiet," warns Harriet. "I don't want to break the painter's concentration."

"Do you see what's going on here?" whispers Harriet.

"Yes," Milton whispers back, "the painter is experimenting. Each time she gets a little better, adding in details like the way the eye sits in the socket. It's as if she's going and really looking at a horse between each attempt."

Harriet nods. "That's right. In that way, she's acting like a modern scientist; always seeking to get things more right each time they come up with an idea. Humans make pictures of how the world and the universe work with words and images. One big part of that is what we call science. Scientists improve on the picture when they can in order to get the best version current knowledge allows."

"So she might be the first scientist?" asks Milton.

"She's certainly one of the first accurate observers of animals (also known now as zoologists) we know about," says Harriet. "But can you see that she is also thinking about her place in the world while she paints? Her composition is part of a much bigger picture, that's about 15 m long. As we saw on our travels, many of these images seem to have some spiritual purpose for the community. I don't want to stop her and ask what the horses mean but she's going to a lot of trouble to paint them, isn't she? They are clearly important to her and her people. So the two go together: doing science and thinking about spiritual matters. In fact, you could say one travels in the slipstream of the other.

"The painter starts by wanting to do something for a larger purpose of religion," explains Harriet, "but ends up serving science too as she improves her observational skills."

Harriet nudges Milton to a different painting. "The second picture I want to show you is part of another big picture. This one is 10 m long, and seems to tell a story of lions hunting bison. But right in the middle of it, look at this bison."

"Amazing!" exclaims Milton. "It seems to be coming right out of the wall! How does she do that?"

"Yes, she's really excelled herself this time," agrees Harriet. "She has used tricks of foreshortening and modelling to make this effect. And do you know something else, Milton?"

"Probably not, so you'd better tell me."

"People used to think the Ancient Greeks were the first to come up with perspective like this in art during the sixth and fifth centuries BC but here's a person doing it tens of thousands of years earlier," says Harriet.

"Our painter here had the same curiosity as the Greeks and came up with some wonderful artistic answers, but these techniques didn't catch on in the wider world," she explains. "The caves were forgotten until very recently so her work didn't go on to inspire perspective drawing in the earliest days of human history."

Harriet ponders for a moment. "No, for that chain reaction of ideas being passed on to others, we have to wait until the Greeks show up. And we would need to see how the big pictures of the world that they created helped them to understand it."

Milton pricks up his ears and whiskers. "You know what, Harriet? I think we need to visit those Greeks before we go home to my master's study."

Harriet smiles and sets a time and date in Ancient Greece. "Funny you should say that, Milton, because I think you're right. We've barely started our quest for answers to our ultimate questions."

"I can't wait!" purrs Milton.

Thanks

Harriet and Milton would like to thank:

Dame Jane Goodall for agreeing to appear in the book in conversation with our time travellers; Professor Stephen Hawking for checking on Harriet's time travel expertise; and Lord Martin Rees for pointing out some of the paradoxes. (Somehow Harriet has managed to get around the one where you aren't supposed to be able to travel back in time in a machine to a date before it was made.)

Where to go to find out more

There are lots of helpful websites that will tell you more about the people, objects, and places mentioned in Milton and Harriet's quest. Here are a few to start you on your own curiosity quest:

Space and time travel: Try NASA's Kids' Club – www.nasa.gov/kidsclub/index.html

Cave paintings: Take the virtual tour of Chauvet – http://archeologie.culture.fr/chauvet/en

Finding awesome fossils: Listen to Maeve Leakey describe her excitement at finding a skull – http://video.nationalgeographic.com/video/curiosity-meave-leakey

Chimpanzees: You can find out lots of exciting facts about them at Jane Goodall's websites – www.janegoodall.org and www.rootsnshoots.org.uk

And you can watch the amazing waterfall dance and hear Jane's description of what might be going on at –

https://youtu.be/jjQCZClpaaY

https://www.youtube.com/watch?v=jjQCZClpaaY

Gorillas: Do you want to visit the big guys of the forest? Then go to https://gorillafund.org/learning-fun/ It includes a personality test to find out which gorilla you are – Harriet is Effie, the matriarch, and Milton is Kundurwanda, the mischievous one!

Orang-utans: Intrigued by these solitary apes? Then visit https://

orangutan.org/ – you can follow the orang-utan of the month and find out other fun facts.

Answer
How many times did you spot the Curiosity Bug? The answer is 23.

Meet the authors

Julia Golding is a multi-award-winning children's novelist, including the *Cat Royal* series and the *Companions Quartet*. Having given up on science at sixteen, she became interested again when she realized just how inspiring science can be. It really does tell the best stories! This is her first experiment with non-fiction but hopefully her collaborators, Roger and Andrew, will prevent any laboratory accidents.

Andrew Briggs is the professor of nanomaterials at the University of Oxford. Nanomaterials just means small stuff. In his laboratory he studies problems like how electricity flows through a single molecule (you can't get stuff much smaller than a single molecule). He is also curious about big questions. He flies aeroplanes, but he has never been in a time travel machine like the one that Harriet and Milton use – yet!

Roger Wagner is an artist who paints power stations and angels (among other things) and has work in collections around the world. He didn't do the drawings for these books, but like Milton and Harriet he wanted to find out how the 'big picture' thinking of artists, was connected to what scientists do. When he met Andrew Briggs the two of them set out on a journey to answer that question. Their journey (which they described in a book called *The Penultimate Curiosity*), was almost (but not quite) as exciting as Milton and Harriet's.

Harriet and Milton continue
their quest in

GREEK
ADVENTURE

– available now!